A TWISTED TWINS STORY

AF094985

Glenda and Gus
Suzi Wieland

Copyright ©2022 by Suzi Wieland
All rights reserved. The reproduction or utilization of this work in whole or in part, by any means, is forbidden without written permission from the author.
This book is a work of fiction. Names, characters, places, and incidents are products of the author's imagination or are used fictitiously. Any resemblance to actual events, locations, or persons, living or dead is entirely coincidental.
Published by Twisted Path Press
First edition June 2022

Chapter One

Nothing tasted better than a gas station burrito when you were starving.

Okay, a lot of things did, but the burrito would have to do for now.

"I'm stuffed to the brim and can't eat another bite." Glenda patted her satisfied stomach, crumpled the wrapper, and tossed it into the trash bag on the seat next to her. She kept her vehicle clean and tidy, unlike her twin brother. "You sure you don't want anything to eat, Gus?"

She glanced in the rearview mirror at him, his legs bent to fit inside the vehicle. Even though the forest green Expedition was roomy, it wasn't roomy enough for a six-foot man to lie flat in the middle row.

He groaned and shifted. Maybe she should adjust his pillow, make him more comfortable before

Glenda and Gus

she hit the road again. But they didn't have too long to go, so might as well continue on.

Glenda removed the plastic from the green tree-shaped air freshener she'd bought in the gas station and slid the string over her mirror. The invigorating pine scent made her want to get to their new home as fast as possible. She put the SUV in drive and pulled out of the parking lot and onto the quiet highway. Only an hour and a half left of their drive.

Her poor brother wasn't feeling well. He'd been queasy when she helped him settle in the SUV this morning, and he had spent most of the time asleep under his blanket. It was the middle of July and quite hot, and Glenda gave him her favorite fuzzy blanket because she had the air on high and didn't want him to be chilly.

Her twin had always been the cold one between them, which was funny. Usually women were the creatures who were always cold. But no, not Glenda. She ran hot.

Unfortunately, Gus had to spend this whole nine-and-a-half-hour drive from Missouri to central Minnesota feeling this way. He didn't even have a chance to eat any of the brownies she'd made for him, but he'd chow them down once he felt better.

Suzi Wieland

Since they'd be living together, she could make brownies and rice krispies and peanut butter cookies for him all the time. When they'd lived in separate homes, she only made him treats about once a week, but now he'd have an endless supply. Gus sure had a sweet tooth, more so than her. But not today because he was feeling ill.

She wouldn't blame him for making her drive the whole way. The sun was bright, and the sky was blue, the perfect day to start a new life in Minnesota lakes country.

They drove along the edge of an immense lake, although she couldn't remember the name posted on the sign. Most of the time she couldn't see it because of the big leafy trees, but every once in a while, they thinned, and she could see a boat skimming across the dark water or the docks dotting the shoreline. Their lake would be nowhere near this size, and she was just fine with that.

"I shall miss Kansas City. Will you?" Glenda asked Gus even though he wouldn't respond. She knew the answer anyway. Gus loved Kansas City, loved the action and activities, especially his baseball team. Lake life would be a big change, but he would appreciate the smell of pine and campfires at night.

Glenda and Gus

Glenda would love fishing the lake and growing her own food on the large lot. And the privacy.

They needed a fresh start, and Gus especially needed a change. They weren't kids anymore, and he needed to slow his life down, stop acting like he was in his twenties. He'd acquired such bad debt from all his gambling, and he'd made so many mistakes, but this was his chance to cast off his baggage and make a change, apologize for all his mistakes and all the hurt he'd caused. He'd taken advantage of their whole family at different times over the years, financially and emotionally, and he needed to make that up to her.

Their new lake place was about forty-five minutes' drive from the closest town with a grocery store, so she'd have to plan trips out better. No more walking out the door and jumping in the car and driving five minutes to buy what you forgot the last time you were at the store. No more running to the coffee shop for a six-dollar latte every morning. She bought a new Keurig, just for this move. A special treat.

But she would miss so many things about Kansas City too. Her quiet house in the peaceful neighborhood next to unobtrusive old-people neighbors. And she'd miss her fellow nurses and the patients in the oncology department, who'd given her a wonderful send-off. Her patients had appreciated her tender touch, the way she'd hold hands with them and explained the things the doctors didn't always take time to, and she'd been good at her job, strong and steady when a dying patient needed that too.

Yes, she'd miss her patients most of all. They were fighters, people who wouldn't give up, and she admired them so and wished she could save each and every one of them. But she had her brother to care for.

She and Gus were only thirty-two, and she considered this year special because they were born thirty-two minutes apart. Apparently she had not wanted to be born like Gus had, so she got stuck, and the whole fiasco ended up with their mom in surgery. Mom always laughed and said she survived two births. One normal with Gus and a c-section with Glenda. But she never blamed Glenda and always said it with a tease in her voice.

Glenda slumped in her seat. Their mom had died of breast cancer when she and Gus were just out of college, and the next year their father had a stroke at the young age of forty-eight and didn't survive. Gus was about all she had left.

Glenda and Gus

Glenda and Gus. Gus and Glenda. Built-in best friends to last for-ev-eh.

Glenda sang the song out loud that her mom taught them when they were little. Twins were special, and Mom was a part of an identical twin set too. Despite the mileage between them, she and her sister had been close until the day Mom died, and Glenda's aunt had been the one there to comfort Glenda the most after they lost their parents.

That job should have been Gus's, but he was a man, and like their father, he wasn't good with that touchy-feely stuff. Sometimes, especially as he grew older, he wasn't as good with the twinning thing either.

"A twin's bond is special, and you two will be best friends for life," Mom said repeatedly as they grew up, whenever they fought about trivial things like who was hogging the bathroom or who received a bigger helping of dessert.

"It'll be strange living with you again, Gus," Glenda said. They hadn't lived together since they were twenty-two. Gus'd had a number of roommates over the years, sometimes buddies and sometimes a girlfriend, but Glenda had mostly lived on her own. The only exception was Shannon, who'd moved out two weeks ago.

Suzi Wieland

Glenda gripped the steering wheel tighter.

Shannon.

Her ex-fiancée.

Her former best friend.

The woman Glenda had wanted to spend her life with.

The fury surged through her, and she battled to keep it inside.

Shannon had betrayed her in the worst way possible, and she was the reason for this whole move. For Glenda to escape the memories, mostly, and the people she'd been friends with. Everybody loved Shannon, including Gus, and Glenda had no desire to sit around listening to people ask her where Shannon went and what had happened between them. Every time she replayed the story of Shannon's betrayal, a sharp pain sliced through her stomach, opening up the deep chasm even wider.

All the camping trips they spent together cuddling in their two-person tent. It meant nothing.

All the bonfires in Glenda's backyard, roasting marshmallows and talking about their future. It meant nothing.

All the trips Glenda took Shannon on: Santorini, Belize, and Bali. It meant nothing.

Glenda and Gus

You, she wanted to shout at the man in the middle seat. But she pressed her lips together and smothered the hot blame. It wasn't all Gus's fault. Yes, he'd been the one to introduce them. Yes, he'd encouraged Glenda to date Shannon. Yes, he'd done his part.

But Glenda had been the one to fully trust Shannon with her heart.

No, the blame could be spread around to many.

The acrid smell of ammonia drifted over the seat and mixed with pine scent. Damn, Gus. Now she'd have to smell that for the rest of the drive. He should have said something when they stopped at the gas station, but no.

At least the leather seat would clean easily. She was used to things like this though from work. What a dumb-dumb she was; she should have been better prepared. Not much she could do now.

She focused on the road again, on the towering green trees and the calm lakes she was zipping by. The home they'd purchased was only one of three cabins on the small lake. It had two bedrooms and wasn't the fanciest of homes, but it was cozy and comfortable. And from where the cabin sat, they would have total privacy. Supposedly, the other two

Suzi Wieland

homes were only used in the summers by rich families who traveled from the Minneapolis area.

Solitude would be wonderful. It had been the whole reason Glenda had bought her previous home with its mature shade trees and private backyard.

She flexed her back, stiff from the long drive. She should turn on the music for Gus, but she was enjoying the quiet hum of the road. Finally, Glenda arrived at a small town and stopped at another gas station. She parked a ways from the door so people wouldn't question her about poor Gus.

"How you doing?" she said after she opened the door.

His eyes opened, and he blinked at her. "Water," he said in a croaky voice. "Where are we?"

Glenda laughed. "I didn't even pay attention to what town this was." All these little places they were passing through were the same. "I'll grab you water. Can you get out and run into the gas station?"

He didn't answer, and she rounded the SUV to the front seat and dug in the cooler for a bottle. Then returned to him.

"You stink, Gus. You should've told me you had to pee. We could've stopped on the road somewhere."

Glenda and Gus

Glenda chuckled again. They'd taken a lot of family road trips when they were kids, and more than once, they'd had to pee alongside the road.

"My head hurts. I feel woozy." He rubbed his forehead and leaned into the seat, and Glenda frowned.

"I have aspirin. Let me find you some." She dug for a pill and gave it to him along with water. While he swallowed it, she studied the trailer behind the Expedition that had all of their possessions. Well, everything they'd brought with. She'd stuffed everything else from her old place into a rental unit. This cabin was partially furnished, and luckily they'd needed little furniture.

"Okay, now." Glenda took the bottle from him when he finished.

She helped him sit all the way up, but when he set his feet outside on the parking lot and tried to stand, he stumbled.

"You want to just wait until we get there? It's probably forty-five minutes at the most." She didn't really want the people inside the gas station to see him like this anyway. They'd probably think Gus was drunk, and she didn't need to call attention to themselves.

Suzi Wieland

"Let's just go." His bloodshot eyes showed his weariness. "Where are we going?"

"Gus." She slapped him on the arm. "You kill me sometimes. I think you need a tish more sleep." At least he didn't complain about being wet.

He'd be no help with the unpacking in this condition, and she'd be doing most of it on her own anyway. She laid him down again and hopped into the front seat.

Her phone buzzed, and she left the SUV in park and checked the text message. Paige. Shannon's little sister. Well, she wasn't really little: she was twenty-one now, but Paige had been like a sister to Glenda too.

You're moving? Why didn't you tell me?

Glenda heard the accusation in the text. Paige had a tough time with Glenda and Shannon's breakup, and maybe Glenda should have told her. But she hadn't talked to many people about this move. Just a few co-workers and friends.

Poor Paige wasn't aware of the real reason for the breakup—Shannon sure as hell hadn't admitted what she'd done, and Glenda refused to crush the girl's love for her sister, to damage that tight sibling bond.

Glenda and Gus

No, Glenda was moving on, and there was no reason to share her pain and exacerbate the situation. Paige knew that things were just not working between Glenda and Shannon, whatever that meant, and that Shannon had moved out of Glenda's home.

She had offered the fresh start to Shannon first, to leave Missouri together, but Shannon had no desire to move to an isolated cabin several states away, to try repair their relationship, and Glenda accepted her decision. She and Shannon were different people, and Glenda couldn't blame Shannon for wanting what she wanted.

Well, she could. And she did. But she'd get over it with time.

Glenda also hadn't told Paige about the cheating, to guard her own heart. She hadn't told anyone else about it, not even Gus; she'd talk to him about it when she was ready.

But mostly she didn't want Paige to hate Shannon.

She tapped her finger on the wheel, thinking. Then glanced at Gus. Telling Paige about the move involved more than a text, and now was not the right time.

Will you be around tonight? Glenda texted back. *Can I give you a call then?*

Suzi Wieland

She waited for a response and then promised to call later. She really didn't want to have this conversation with Paige, because so much of it involved her sister, and Glenda would have to keep some of the details secret. And she just hoped Paige wouldn't call her on her lies.

Chapter Two

Glenda pulled onto the road again. She wanted to drive a hundred miles per hour to the waiting cabin, but she stuck to the speed limit, and the drive passed quickly.

Her time estimate had been correct. About fifteen minutes on the main highway and then fifteen minutes of gravel. Their cabin was all the way at the end of the lake road, trees going on forever, and the driveway was long enough that the house was hidden by the silent sentries, the pine trees and birch and oaks.

Nobody would be driving by their place to get anywhere. No cars beeping, no low roar of semi-trucks on the interstate. Here, the trees would filter out the world.

She stared at their new home out the front window as Gus snored lightly. The thick trees hugged the one-story red cedar log cabin with a green roof and green trim. She climbed out and strolled around the small cabin and past the large shed where she planned to work on her big project. The leaves on the ground from the previous autumn rustled, and a squirrel shot out and ran for a tree.

"Don't worry, buddy. I won't hurt you." She tried to follow his path, but he disappeared into the leaves. This place would be filled with wildlife, bunnies and fox and deer. She couldn't wait.

She rounded the cabin to the lakeside and stepped onto the deck that lined the front, plenty of room for a few chairs and a grill. And these windows would allow in so much light inside; she could imagine sitting here for hours enjoying the view.

She had about fifty feet of grass to the water's edge, and the smooth surface stretched out in front of her. Glenda sighed in contentment. Goose Lake. Her own private oasis. It had a silly name that was shared with tons of other lakes in Minnesota, but she didn't care about that. And the fresh pine smell energized her. No exhaust, no stagnant river water, no pollution from the factories, and no smell of Aldunio's Pizzeria. She had loved that place, but passing by it every day on her walk to work made her tire of pizza.

Glenda and Gus

She stepped through the grass, which needed mowing, to the edge of the shore and looked into the calm, clear water. A dragonfly swooped over the surface and settled on the dock extending into the lake. She had no beach, but none was needed.

Birds chirped in the trees, her only neighbors, and she longed to dig out her bird identification book, but she'd wait. She had much to do.

The next cabin was about a mile back the winding road of the s-shaped lake, and their home was not visible from here. She was utterly alone, standing under the stunning colors in the sky, the oranges and blues and purples of the sunset framing the lake. Every night she would be able to see this beautiful sight. Every night she'd be able to sit outside and count the stars. All of them! She was living in a postcard.

A bench swing… that was something she'd need.

She was so lucky.

No, she'd been smart.

When Mom died of cancer, her insurance policy had been paid out to her father. And then when he died, she and Gus inherited the money from their estates. All told, it had been over a million dollars each.

Suzi Wieland

Glenda had socked ninety-five percent of her money away into investments while Gus had quit his job, bought a fancy house, and gambled his money away. Shortly after, he'd had to find a job again because his money was gone. He'd been living paycheck to paycheck, spending above his means all these years, and he'd gotten into trouble.

He just made the worst decisions sometimes, horrible mistakes, but Glenda still loved him—they had a special bond.

She wanted to share this picture with him, but even if she woke him up, he wouldn't enjoy it much. He'd be cranky and snap at her because he wasn't feeling well, and because, well… that was Gus.

No. They had lots of time to spend together in the coming days, and she just wanted to enjoy this moment herself.

*

Dusk blanketed the woods, along with the singing of the insects and frogs, and Glenda couldn't wait to see the star-speckled sky. She'd need to buy a book on constellations, maybe even a telescope.

Thank god she'd picked up firewood. The surrounding woods held plenty of kindling but no big logs. They'd need an axe too. She had a list going

Glenda and Gus

of the things she'd need to buy. The SUV and trailer sat, still full. Tomorrow she'd tackle the moving-in part, but tonight was bonfire time. Gus was sleeping in bed already. That party-pooper. So she was on her own.

Glenda stoked the fire, and flickering orange flames burst from the pit and floated to the sky. She took a deep breath, enjoying the smell from the pit that sat halfway between the water and the cabin.

Okay. Glenda perched on the edge of her seat. Now that she was in a good mood, she should call Paige. She swiped her phone and waited for Paige to answer.

"You're right. You're right," Glenda said as soon as soon as Paige picked up. "I should've told you."

"It would've been nice to say goodbye." Paige sounded wounded, but she'd get over it. Perhaps Glenda's decision had been a bad one; she should've said goodbye to Paige in person, but this last week had been so hectic, years of her life in Kansas City to box up and move.

"I'll make it up to you. I'll be totally settled in by next summer, and you can come visit." She meant it. Just because her relationship with Shannon was over didn't mean she had to write Paige off too. She wasn't sure if the visit would happen though. Yes, Paige was upset Glenda had left so suddenly, but she was twenty-one, she was in college, and she had her own busy life to lead. She'd already accepted that Glenda and Shannon would never get back together again.

"That'd be cool. Where did you move anyway?"

"Minnesota. I'll text you a picture of where I am when we're done talking." She glanced at the SUV, which held many of her possessions, including the one memento of her time with Shannon that she couldn't bear to give up. "So, um. You talked to Shannon earlier?"

"No, she just texted. She was heading to St. Louis for the weekend. Visiting a college friend."

A college friend. Code for her secret liaisons that she'd used on Glenda too. Glenda should've figured that out a long time ago, but she'd been too naïve, too trusting.

She was a dumb-dumb.

Glenda pushed down the pain. She was over Shannon. At least she wanted to be. Getting over someone was easier said than done.

She pasted a smile on her face, even though Paige couldn't see it. "Well, I hope she has fun."

Glenda and Gus

"So I want to see your new place." The excitement was back in Paige's voice, and Glenda's phone started ringing. Glenda laughed and switched to the video call Paige was trying to start. Luckily there was still enough light. She focused the camera on the cabin.

"This is it. My new little oasis." She'd only been here a few hours, but already she was in love with her cabin.

Paige sucked in a hard breath. "It's so cute. But why Minnesota?"

Lots of reasons. But mostly one.

"I just needed distance. Some perspective. And this was the right place."

"Well, I love it. And I want to see the inside now too."

Paige was one of the things she would miss from her old life, but even if Glenda had not moved, she would be seeing her less.

The grand tour didn't last too long, and Glenda skipped Gus's room so she didn't disturb him. There just wasn't a whole lot to see now, not until she decorated the empty pine walls.

"It'll look really different when you come out next summer, I bet." The empty cabin felt so lonely, but soon she'd make it warm and cozy. The previous owners had left the furniture and major appliances but nothing else. "It'll look like a typical cabin in the woods. Deer heads and fish on the wall." Plus, she had a terrific idea that she wanted to try to spruce up the cabin. She wasn't sure when she would get started; it totally depended on Gus.

"You and those stuffed deer." Paige laughed. "They give me the creeps."

Glenda's former house didn't have the space or the style for the collection her dad had left her, but the majority of the mounts would fit into this new home. Perfectly. Taxidermy was an unusual hobby, but here in these woods, it'd fit right in. And she could practice this new hobby in peace. She was excited to begin her first project.

"You'd get used to it." Glenda was proud of the deer she'd shot when she was a kid. But Gus wasn't a huge fan of their dad's collection either.

Glenda strolled into the living area. "I don't know what my favorite part is." She raised the camera to show off the ceiling with its wood beams and the stone fireplace. And the built-in shelves she'd fill with pictures and other items.

"That fireplace will be warm and cozy in the winter. I bet it gets cold." Paige faked a shiver.

Glenda and Gus

"Probably." Glenda laughed. As rustic as this place appeared, everything was well taken care of, and she had everything she needed, so she wasn't going without anything.

She headed toward the front door, and something light thumped in Gus's room.

"Hey, Paige. I need to pee. I'm going to set you down for a minute, and I'll be right back."

She set the phone on the kitchen counter and muted it, then opened Gus's door. He lay flat on his back, his arms at his sides, the thin blanket covering him.

Still out. But his pillow lay on the floor. She picked it up and lifted his head, stuffing it underneath. Because she was a good sister like that. Always thinking of her brother.

She just wished she could say the same for him.

Then she returned to her call with Paige.

Chapter Three

Glenda was up bright and early. Sunrise here came a tish sooner than in Kansas City, and she'd left the bedroom curtains open to enjoy her first day in her new home. Since the living area and kitchen faced the lake, she didn't have that view, but the swaying trees and sky were still visible out the window. She crawled out of bed, put her robe on, and padded to the kitchen.

The water surface was glass, and mourning doves cooed in the trees. *Mourning* doves wasn't really a fitting name in her opinion. Their calls filled her soul with peace, and she looked forward to hearing them more often.

She'd need no big pontoon or speedboat, but maybe a small motorboat for fishing would do.

Every year until they were teenagers, Glenda and Gus's parents brought them to Blue Springs Campground for one week. They had an RV but also

Glenda and Gus

had a tent so Glenda and her dad could rough it. Granted, they had the RV right next to them, but sleeping closer to nature was fun. Gus always stayed inside the RV with Mom though. Sometimes he'd fish with Glenda and their father, but he never helped clean the fish, never scraped the scales off or gutted one. He was too squeamish.

Glenda let out a soft laugh. Gus was like Mom in that way. Glenda loved her mother more than anything, but Mom was not an outdoorsy type. Dad was the one who taught her to filet a fish and grill it on a campfire. He was the one who taught her how to fire a shotgun and skin a deer.

Mom taught her about gardens, about tending to delicate plants and growing food they could enjoy all summer long. She taught her how to can those foods, and next summer Glenda would till the ground and put a garden in. It'd be nowhere as large as her mom's was—she'd have to clear trees for that, but it would be a start.

Maybe Gus could help fertilize the garden.

She laughed. Ahh, Gus. He'd never enjoyed mowing the lawn or gardening.

She had so many projects to fill her time, but this one with Gus would take priority. Then she'd make improvements to the cabin. Adding handles to the cabinetry was one, paint on the walls inside was another. Easy things.

Glenda finally climbed out of bed and dressed. Time to haul in a few loads from the trailer and make breakfast for her and Gus. She passed his room and peeked inside, but his eyes were still closed, and he snored. He should be feeling better today.

"Glenda and Gus. Gus and Glenda. Built-in best friends to last for-ev-eh." She sung the tune softly as she carried in boxes and set them in the middle of the floor of the living room. Unpacking would take time, but she had all the time in the world. Luckily she'd been able to bring food from her kitchen in Kansas City, so she wouldn't have to hit the grocery store for several days. She'd run out of milk by then, but Gus was the only one who'd complain about that.

She brought in the buck earlier, the one she'd shot at seventeen. Her dad had been so impressed with the deer that he'd had the head stuffed for her so she could mount it on the wall. It had stayed in her parents' house until after he died, and then it, and the rest of his collection, went to her since Gus didn't want it.

Glenda and Gus

She couldn't wait to hang them all. She had a special fish chosen for Gus too, the largemouth bass she'd hung in his room.

She unpacked the box with the basic kitchen necessities, silverware and her favorite pots and pans, and got to work scrambling eggs and frying bacon. Using the microwave wasn't her favorite way to make bacon, but Gus might wake up at any moment, so she wanted to have breakfast ready on the first morning in their new home.

The appliances in the kitchen were fairly new and solid, and she doubted she'd have to replace any soon. No garbage disposal was a big change though, and she'd have to get used to that.

She might need a few other things, and she'd give it a month before deciding what she truly needed. She had plenty of money, but she'd always been frugal like her mother. Her father hadn't exactly been a big spender, but somehow Mom and Dad produced one child whose bank account was rarely full because he spent all his money on frivolous things. No matter how much their parents helped Gus, he couldn't handle his money.

Glenda scrambled eggs and cooked bacon and then loaded the eggs onto a plate. She already had one cup of coffee and had started on her second.

Suzi Wieland

"Glenda!" Gus yelled, his voice stronger today. "Get in here?"

"Give me a minute to fill your plate," she called back, keeping her voice light. Grumpy Gus would need cheering up this morning. She salted and peppered the eggs on both her plate and his, snatched some bacon—more for Gus—set the bottles of water on the tray along with the food, and strolled to Gus's bedroom.

"What's going on?" Gus struggled on the bed, tugging on the padded leather restraints that held him in place. Only the best for her Gus. His bed was the only big piece of furniture that she brought with. A metal frame bed like the type they used in psychiatric facilities. "What did you do to me? Where are we?"

"Hold on a minute." She set the tray down and walked to the window and opened the curtains, allowing in the morning sun that filtered through the trees. "I'll loosen the restraints as long as you calm down." She hadn't given him much room to wiggle, but if he was good, she could relax them.

"What the hell, Glen. What are you doing? Let me out of here." Gus's face was red from exertion, and she hoped he didn't upset his stomach. He'd

Glenda and Gus

been on a lot of drugs the last twenty-four hours or so.

She stopped beside his bed, just out of reach, and he yanked on the handcuffs and jerked at his feet. His feet had even less give than his hands.

"Stop that." She shook a finger at him. "You'll just give yourself more bruises."

A few dark spots dotted his skin from when she'd dragged him inside last night. She hadn't meant to bump him, but his drugged body was dead weight in her hands.

She returned to the food on the chair beside his bed. "Now, if you settle down, I shall loosen your restraints so you can eat breakfast. I made bacon and scrambled eggs." She pointed to the food on the plate. "It's getting cold."

His glare deepened, but he stopped struggling and leaned into the pillows, his jaw tight. For the first time, she wondered if he would actually apologize for his transgressions.

She would see.

She waited another minute and then adjusted the strap on his left hand. He was a righty, like her, so eating would take longer this way, but he'd be less apt to attack her.

Suzi Wieland

She set the paper plate with a plastic fork on his lap, gave him a water bottle, and backed up. It might be awkward to drink from the bottle, but he'd figure it out.

Gus scarfed down the breakfast as quickly as he could while Glenda ate slowly. She liked to enjoy her food, as Gus usually did too, but he was probably starving. He hadn't been able to eat much with as drugged up as he was yesterday.

"Can I have more?" he asked, very civilly. She wasn't used to such politeness from him.

She stood and reached her hand out. The paper plate had been a good idea so then he couldn't fling it at her. She took the plate, retreated to the kitchen to dish up, and returned to him.

He ate again, watching her with suspicious eyes, but didn't say anything until he finished and held up his plate and fork to her. She'd need to give him a sponge bath soon. She'd changed his peed-on clothes last night, but he still smelled sweaty and musty.

"Glen," Gus said with a warning tone.

As if he should be the one speaking to her like that. He'd been the one to hurt her; he'd caused her much pain.

Glenda and Gus

He was her twin, for mercy's sake, a bond that shouldn't be broken.

She slumped in her chair, the hollowness returning. He'd stolen her happiness, her future. Twins were supposed to love one another, not destroy each other.

"I know about Shannon." She gripped the arms of the chair tightly.

Shannon, the woman Glenda had loved more than anything. The woman who had agreed to spend her life with Glenda. The woman who was sleeping with her brother.

Gus averted his eyes, his face flaming red.

He should be ashamed! He'd hit on Shannon, cajoled her, talked her into sleeping with him. Then had kept it up for months right under Glenda's nose.

Right in her home.

They'd both lied to her, wounded her badly.

"It didn't mean anything," he huffed.

"Didn't mean anything? She was my fiancée, Gus. You are my brother. How could you hurt me?"

Shannon had tried the same excuse. *It didn't mean anything. It was just sex.*

The worst thing was all those times when she'd returned from work and would find Gus stretched out on her sofa, she'd thought how wonderful it was that her twin, the most important person in her life, her only family left, got along so well with her fiancée.

Well, they got along so well because they'd been having sex for months.

Never had she considered it. He usually had a half-drank beer beside him, like he'd been there for twenty minutes. Often Shannon was in the kitchen making dinner. She'd bring Glenda a drink and leave to let brother and sister catch up on the day's events.

Poor naïve Glenda had no clue. But Shannon would never hurt anyone else again. And neither would Gus.

He had been quiet, and Glenda focused on him again, but he wasn't looking at her. His gaze was trained on the largemouth bass mounted on the wall behind her, like he hadn't seen it until now. He hated that thing with a passion, the gaping mouth and pokey fin. When he was a kid, he thought the bass would sneak into his room at night and gobble up his toes.

Gus blinked and shook his head. "I'm sorry. I didn't want to do it, but one time I stopped by, and you weren't home, and she flashed me. Then she like stripped down, and it was so hard to say no. You know how weak I am." He pleaded at her with his

Glenda and Gus

big brown eyes. Eyes that Shannon could not say no to either. Glenda wasn't so sure Gus really was sorry though. He just wanted out of the cuffs. "She was no good for you."

"I know." Glenda sighed. "In the end, she admitted it." Shannon had begged and pleaded for forgiveness, but Glenda didn't have it in her. Not after all these years. Shannon had always been a flirt, but Glenda thought she'd been an honest woman.

Gus cleared his throat. "Can you just let me out, please?"

Maybe she should've suspected he would sleep with Shannon; maybe she should've known. In high school he'd slept with a girl Glenda had been crushing on. She hadn't been a lesbian anyway, but Gus had known how much Glenda liked her, and then he dumped her after two weeks.

And college was just a repeat of high school. Glenda had dated a woman who decided that she wasn't really a lesbian after all, and who did she run to the moment she turned straight?

To Gus, of course. Gus, who she'd joked about being so hot.

And most of the other girls Glenda had dated… They'd been awesome, and they'd been faithful, but the way Gus looked at them creeped them out. The jokes he made about them hooking up after they ditched Glenda. They didn't like it and refused to be around him, not that Glenda could blame them, and since she lived with Gus in that house on campus their parents had rented for them, she had little choice. She'd asked him to stop with the jokes, but he never did.

And then there were her friends that he'd driven away too, friends he dated and cheated on and hurt them so badly that they refused to remain friends with Glenda. She'd begged him many times to leave her friends alone, but he repeated his actions several times.

Gus stared at her, waiting.

He'd be waiting a long time.

"You hurt me, Gus. It's too late." The empty hole in her heart yearned to be filled, but this time she wouldn't depend on another woman to fulfill her.

"It's never too late. Shannon isn't important to me. You are." His words rushed out, which meant he was lying. And besides, he had a funny way of showing that. "Please, Glen, just let me go, and we can talk. I know I was a jackass. And mean to you. I've been a rotten brother. And I'll tell Shannon we're through." He hung his head, and she rolled her

Glenda and Gus

eyes at the faker. She'd been dumb to think he might truly be remorseful. He'd never change.

"You want to tell Shannon you're through?" Glenda asked. She could grant him that.

His head popped up with the slightest bit of hope. "Yes, I will. Right now. And then after that, we can get breakfast."

She didn't bother reminding him that he just ate.

She stalked out of the room and wheeled in her new blue cooler she'd bought just for this move.

"Okay, go ahead." She pointed to the cooler, and he frowned.

"Go ahead and what? Where's my phone?" He scanned the room frantically, wiggling around in his restraints.

"Go ahead and tell her." Glenda patted the cooler. "I don't want to open it. She kind of smells."

"Sh-Sh-Sh-Shannon?" A white curtain fell across Gus's face, and his lips trembled. The room grew deadly silent. "She's in the cooler?"

"Yes, Gus. Well, just her head." Glenda dropped the handle and perched on the cooler. The rest of her body was scattered among random dumpsters in Kansas City.

"She's dead?" Gus's voice cracked, and he flopped into his pillow. His head tipped to the ceiling, his lids filling with tears.

Oh no. Had he actually loved her? Glenda almost laughed. Now, wouldn't that be funny. If the first person Gus had truly loved—his sister's fiancée, mind you—had been two-timing him too. But Glenda wasn't sure Gus was capable of that kind of love; he'd been on a road to eternal bachelorhood, never settling for one person. He was too selfish and spoiled. He might just be too overcome with emotion now, trying to process.

She had to give him the complete picture so he understood.

"She lied to me too. Last year I discovered she slept with one of her co-workers, and she promised it would never happen again. I believed her." Glenda gave a wry laugh. What a dumb-dumb she'd been. "But then, after I found out about you, I found out about even more too. Did you know she was cheating on you too?" Glenda waited until Gus shook his head.

Shannon was a serial cheater. She would've cheated on whomever she ended up with next. And the person after that. Serial cheaters didn't stop

Glenda and Gus

unless someone put a stop to them, and Glenda was saving others from the pain she'd experienced.

"She had two others on the side," Glenda continued. "One man and one woman. Just flings. The thing I can't figure out was what you two were planning. I mean, she and I were engaged, so would the three of us grow old together as some wild throuple that I didn't know about?"

Glenda snorted. Of course that wouldn't have happened. Shannon would've broken it off with him too when she grew bored.

"It wasn't like that." Gus tugged on his restraints again. "I was just stringing her along. I knew she would marry you, and we'd break it off."

He was lying; she could hear it in his voice. He'd had real feelings for Shannon, just like Glenda had, but she scammed them both. At this point, Glenda couldn't gather any empathy for her heartbroken brother.

"Know what, Gus?" Glenda stood, dusted off her pants, and picked up the cooler handle. "I have a lot to do today. So much to unpack."

"Unpack. Wait. Where are we?" He glanced out the window to the wall of trees. If he was standing in front of the glass, he could probably see down the driveway, but he couldn't from the bed.

Suzi Wieland

"Let me know if your bag needs emptying." She motioned to the lump under the bed next to his body, and he tugged the blanket away. She almost laughed. He hadn't even noticed that he had the catheter inside him. She'd been a tish dumb with it actually. She should've put it in before the trip, but she'd been rushed and wasn't thinking straight.

He'd have no more issues with peeing himself now. Bowel movements would be an issue though.

She walked away, rolling the cooler with her and ignoring his yelling. She had too much to do. She needed to put everything away so that she could start on her project, and listening to Gus's whining would grate on her nerves. She also had to figure out what to do with Shannon. And the cooler, which would need to be destroyed thanks to the smell. Glenda's new life was beginning, and she wanted to move on.

Glenda slipped outside to the spacious shack behind the house. This was one of the reasons that sold her on this property, along with the almost complete seclusion she had out here. The shed needed a good dusting before she organized her new tools in here for her new hobby. She had everything she needed in the trailer.

She stood in the ray of sunlight streaming in through the shed window. This was the life, so

Glenda and Gus

peaceful and calm. If only she'd moved someplace like this years ago, she would've never met Shannon, wouldn't have had her heart broken.

Perhaps she and Gus shared that now, broken hearts. With time, those emotions would fade, and she would be happy again.

A door slammed, and Glenda startled. What was that? Had Gus escaped? Impossible. The restraints bound him to the bed. Her heart battered her chest.

She rounded the cabin and stopped short. A woman was leaning into the back end of a car in the gravel drive, trying to wrangle something from the back seat. Glenda scampered over to the woman, who she now recognized as the realtor she'd worked with. Everything was done online, Maxine showing her the property on video messaging, sending her the keys when the paperwork was finalized.

Gus wasn't yelling anymore, but if he realized someone else was here, he'd start back up again. Maxine should have called.

But Glenda should have seen this coming. Maxine had been so lovely, and they'd spent time chatting about their families when Glenda was looking at this property. She knew all about Maxine's teenagers and the husband who was an elementary school principal.

"Good morning." Glenda threw a smile on her face.

Maxine spun around, the basket in her arms. "Glenda. Hello. It's so nice to meet you in person. Are you settling in?" She raised the basket full of oranges and apples and grapes and other fruit. "I brought this to you and wanted to say welcome to the community."

Oh, that was so sweet. Maxine wasn't that much older than Glenda, and she could see them becoming friends.

Glenda took the fruit basket, keeping herself between the house and the woman. "Thank you. What a nice welcome."

Glenda wasn't a grapefruit person, but Gus would eat it. She glanced at the house, but it was quiet. She didn't know for how long though. He could let loose a yell at any moment, and the cabin was too small to muffle the sound.

And she didn't want to have to clean up another mess.

No, she needed to get Maxine out of here and now. Before Gus ruined everything again.

Chapter Four

"Glenda," Gus yelled from his room. "I need you."

She paused with her sticky hand on the sharp knife, halfway through the deep pink flesh bleeding over the wood cutting board. "Just a moment, Gus. I need to finish up here."

She loved how she could stand at the granite counter, looking out at her view of the lake while she worked in her kitchen. The view at her new home was her favorite thing.

It was almost twelve-thirty now. Maxine had thrown everything off-schedule for the day, but Glenda was working fast to catch up.

Glenda sliced through the quartered watermelon and cut away the rind. Then she picked out the seeds so it'd be easier for Gus to eat.

That Maxine was so kind, bringing the fruit basket for her. They'd stood in the driveway and spoken a few minutes, and then Glenda made excuses for getting settled and asked Maxine if they could meet at a coffee shop sometime.

She finished with the seeds, scraped them into her hand with the knife, and tossed them into the garbage basket.

"Almost done," Glenda called again. She grabbed the plate with the sandwich and slid watermelon onto it. Then set the plate on the tray along with the bottle of water and straw, and she carried it to Gus's room.

Oh no.

Glenda paused in the doorway, her hip about to nudge the door open, and she cringed at the putrid stank. Gus should have mentioned that he was going to have a bowel movement.

She returned the tray to the kitchen and strode into his room, now in nurse mode.

"Gus, what did you do?" The poop stink clogged her nose, but she didn't show her disgust. Instead she opened the window for some fresh air.

"You don't let me out to use the bathroom," he growled. He jerked on his restraints, his fiery eyes tearing into her.

"You don't need a bathroom. You have a catheter. And you should have called me, so we could have done this together."

Glenda and Gus

"What?" he sputtered, his face red. "You'd bring me to the bathroom so I could take a shit in front of you?"

Glenda's head tilted to the side. No, that wasn't her plan, but she'd explain that all after she cleaned him up. She strode to the side of the bed and considered the best way to handle this. His legs were tied up, and she couldn't remove his pants. And he'd kick at her if she released the binds from his legs. And she needed to change the bed too now.

This was all one big mess.

"Okay, Gus." She laid her hand on his knee, and he jerked back.

"Stop touching me, you crazy bitch."

Glenda gasped. She was not the crazy one here.

Crazy was thinking you could sleep with your twin sister's fiancée and that she'd never find out. Crazy was breaking their twin bond in the most horrendous way.

"Would you like to sit in your shit all day? Would you like me to show you pictures of babies and their diaper rash, their red flaming skin?" She got her voice under control. She was a nurse, and she could temper her feelings.

Gus sunk back onto the bed, his bravado fizzling away. "No," he whispered.

Suzi Wieland

First she would clean him up, then she would let him eat, and after that, she'd sedate him so she could properly change the bed and slip him into new clothes.

"I'll be right back." She scuttled out of the room to gather her supplies. A scissors to cut off the pants, a garbage bag, and a couple blankets. Then she retrieved a bunch of paper towels, a bowl of warm water, and old rags.

Gus eyed her wearily. She didn't understand why he didn't trust her. She'd spent years caring for cancer-ridden patients, many who sometimes lost control of their bodies. At least with them, they didn't choose to poop their pants.

"Just let me go to the bathroom," he begged.

"We both know I can't allow that." She started snipping the thin pants he wore.

"What are you doing?" He jiggled around, and she stopped, halfway up his leg.

"We need to remove these pants." She pushed down on his leg. "Now hold still so I don't cut you." She was careful to avoid the tube for the catheter.

"No, Glen. Stop." Gus clamped onto the handrails, his body stiff, his face beet red.

"I am a nurse. How many people do you think I've seen naked before? We all look the same

Glenda and Gus

underneath our clothes." And how did he think she'd inserted the catheter?

He fell silent, his head turned away from her as she worked. The smell worsened with his pants opened up. She finished cutting them and sliced off his underwear.

She was a professional, and she would never make fun of his small penis. She had to admit she'd been surprised. He'd been sedated when she inserted the catheter and didn't witness her reaction, but Gus was much smaller than she'd imagined. With all the women he'd been with and the way some of those women talked, she'd imagined him to be a big stud.

But he wasn't.

He was below average actually.

She would not tell him that though. She was a good sister.

She had him roll on his side to slide the pants off. Luckily the poop had not soaked through to the sheet, but she'd still wash it up so he could have a clean bed. He lay there, his body stiff. She supposed she would be the same if she were in this situation, but Gus was not a nurse. He did not work in the cancer ward with desperate patients; he did not have a tender hand and soft heart like she did.

Suzi Wieland

"This is wrong," Gus said as she wiped his butt like a child.

"It's also wrong to sleep with your sister's fiancée," she reminded him.

He didn't respond.

She finished up her job with no thanks from Gus, and after washing up, she retrieved his plate, minus the pudding, which she'd keep near her chair. The pudding that now contained a sedative to knock him out.

"Lunchtime," Glenda sang out.

Again, no thank you from him.

She sat with him as he ate, but he refused to look at her. He didn't even appreciate the seeded watermelon. Finally, he finished, and she took his tray and reached down to grab the pudding.

"You know they'll figure out what happened. The cops." Gus set his fiery eyes on her, as if to intimidate her.

She laughed. He had no power anymore.

"No, they won't. Nobody will even notice you're gone for a few days." She abandoned the pudding and returned to the kitchen drawer to remove two phones. She would be taking care of these soon but wanted to show Gus. She held up the

Glenda and Gus

phones for him to see: the first in its practical gray case and the second in its glittery gold case.

"My phone." Gus gave her a lovely smile. "Can I use it? I'm so bored. I have nothing to do except stare out the window."

"I'm not a dumb-dumb. You can watch the squirrels in the trees. I know they play out there sometimes." She flicked it on and brought up the text messages. "Shall I read these for you?" She didn't wait for a response from him. "Shannon: *You sure you want to go to St. Louis with me and Tishel?* Gus: *Hell, yeah.* Shannon: *Okay. Be ready at seven.* Gus: *I'll be ready and waiting, babe.*" Glenda had added the babe because Gus often used it in his texts to Shannon.

He frowned at her now. "What the fuck is all that?"

Glenda shook her head. Her brother was the denser of the two of them. "That's you planning your trip to St. Louis with Shannon's friend. Nobody will even think about you for days. I texted a few of your friends. And I texted Paige too for Shannon."

Which was when *Shannon* had told Paige about Glenda moving.

The crevasses in his forehead grew deeper, and his lip curled into a sneer. "It won't work. They're probably tracking our phones right now."

Suzi Wieland

"I'm not worried." Glenda chuckled again. After sending off the text messages that day, she'd removed the cards from the phone, shut off cellular data, and put them on airplane mode. And she'd destroy these two phones next. "I'm sure your St. Louis trip is a lot of fun. You just won't return."

And the ironic thing was that Gus hated St. Louis. The city was *boring*, and he avoided it at all costs.

"Who the fuck is Tishel?"

"Shannon's friend. Imaginary, of course. She was driving you." Glenda was proud of her ingenuity on that one. She bought a phone with cash, one that couldn't be traced to her, and texted Shannon about the trip.

"Let me the fuck out of here!" Gus yelled at her and yanked on his restraints so hard she worried he might dislocate a wrist. His checks grew red, his forehead shiny. "Help, help!"

But nobody would hear him.

She let him have his temper tantrum, and finally he settled down, huffing and puffing. At this point, she should refuse to let him have his pudding, but she needed to knock him out so she could change his bed.

Glenda and Gus

She reached for the pudding and stood. "Are you done? Because if you're done, I'll give you the pudding. But if you're not, I'll just shut the door and let you continue on."

Giving him the pudding was a risk. He might throw it at her or at the wall. But pudding was one of his favorite desserts, so she was banking on him wanting the treat.

His eyes narrowed into slits, his mouth a matching thin line.

"Good boy." Glenda smiled. She walked to the bed and set the pudding in front of him. Then she turned around to leave. Another risk. And she hoped that dish wouldn't come flying at her head.

Chapter Five

Glenda spent three days carrying boxes, unpacking, and settling in. Her arms and back ached, and she needed a good massage, but she wanted everything done. It would've been so nice if Gus had been able to help her, but despite what he said about him being good, he wouldn't be if she let him go.

She was proud of all she had accomplished. Hard work really did have its rewards.

Simplicity was the theme of her new life, and she'd left so much behind, donated many of her belongings and furniture so other people could use it. And the leftovers were in that storage shed.

She passed by the closed door to his room. Boy, the begging and whining and pleading and swearing; she'd thought Gus would've been a bigger man than this. She only visited him a few times during the day, when he needed food and his bag changed, and the

Glenda and Gus

whole bowel movement thing. At least he wasn't pooping in his clothes anymore.

She would continue to be his happy nurse, to play the role for him. She did feel bad that he had nothing to do, but she couldn't allow him a phone or computer, and she didn't have the TV or internet set up yet anyway.

She didn't need any of that right now. She had her big project to think about, to get moving on. Yesterday she unpacked her new supplies in her special workshop, the shed. Everything was organized and ready to go. She'd spent a lot of money to buy everything she needed and wanted to make sure she wasn't in the middle of everything and realized she was missing something.

"Morning," she said when she entered his room. He eyed her as she set his food on the bed and sat in the extra chair. "Thank you for being quiet last night."

His shoulders drooped. The bags under his eyes had grown darker, like he'd aged ten years.

"Glen, this is enough now," he said softly. "You can let me go. Where are we even? I can't hear anything except for the birds and bugs." He pushed the eggs on the plate around with his fork and then blinked up at her with those sad puppy-dog eyes.

Suzi Wieland

She sucked in a sharp breath. Why didn't she think of this before? She should've been playing music for him, for a distraction, if nothing else. Oh well, too late now. He wouldn't be stuck in this room after today.

"We're in Minnesota at our new lake cabin." She grinned. "The seller was motivated since they hadn't lived here in a while, so I was able to move in right away. You should see the lake. It's so beautiful." She'd spent a few hours yesterday swimming in the cool waters, and she couldn't wait to hit the store in town to buy a floaty. She could show him a few pictures, but that might be mean, teasing him with what he couldn't have.

"Minnesota," he gruffed. "Where the hell in Minnesota?"

Glenda's head snapped up. He'd been so polite just moments ago.

"North of Minneapolis." A ways out of the city actually. But he wasn't familiar with the small towns around anyway. She hadn't been.

He tossed his fork on the plate as if he wouldn't be eating the delicious breakfast she'd prepared for him.

"And how long do you intend to punish me like this?" His voice grew harder.

Glenda and Gus

"Not much longer, in fact. Soon, you will be free."

"Oh, thank god." His shoulders relaxed, and she hid her glee. She couldn't wait to tell him the next part. She had to admit that she only wanted to tell him to see his reaction. He wouldn't appreciate the art aspect of her project, but the subject was the intriguing part.

Gus was her inspiration, her motivation.

"First, I have to prepare things. Then I'll tell you my plan." She stood and strode out. Her bag rested on the table with the syringe inside.

Yes, she was being a tish dramatic with the syringe when she could give him the liquid sedative, but she didn't care anymore. Gus had been the one to cause the drama most of their lives, and now she wanted to be the one to have fun.

She carried the bag into the bedroom and perched on the edge of her seat.

"Don't you just love that big-mouth bass?" Glenda asked, waving at the fish on the wall.

His face twisted up. "You know I don't."

"Dad spent a lot of money on his taxidermy. You should see the other room. The deer and the fish and the pheasants and ducks. Dad had so many of them, and I can't put them all up, but I'll rotate them in and out."

"What a fucking waste," he spit, but then he noticed Glenda's hard scowl. "I'm sure they look great in this cabin though. You're better at decorating than he was." Gus gave her a wide smile, and she almost laughed. He was not being sincere in the least.

"They are spectacular. Dad would be proud."

"Dad would fu—" he started but snapped his mouth shut. "Dad would be proud of what you've done. He'd love visiting this cabin, wouldn't he?"

"He would," Glenda gushed. He would've appreciated the solitude and the lake as much as she did. Losing her parents at such a young age hit her hard, and she wished she'd had the chance to share this cabin with him and her mom.

"Actually, I'd like to see it. Can you let me out?" He pasted that silly smile on his face.

"You'll get out soon enough." She dropped her bag on the chair with a thunk. Time for her big reveal. "The reason I bought this place was because of how secluded it is. There's nobody around for miles. Okay, one house a mile away and then a second, but after that it's a ways to the next house. It's so beautiful here. You'll love it."

Glenda and Gus

"I'm not staying. I'm going back to Missouri. City life is more my thing." His voice was strained, and by the way he was gripping the handrails, she knew he was trying to keep from yelling at her. She admired his restraint.

"Right outside that wall is a large shed. There's no garage here, but maybe by this fall, I'll have one built. The shed is the perfect workplace, and I have the tools and everything I need for my taxidermy project."

"You're going to stuff a deer? Or a fish? Have you been fishing?" He looked incredulous.

It was a big project to tackle for her first, but she had all the time in the world. And she should explain to him that it wasn't really just stuffing an animal. Taxidermy was complicated, and she'd watched a ton of videos and read many books. She had the patience to do research on things like that, especially after she broke up with Shannon.

"Not, a deer, dumb-dumb. I have bigger fish to fry." She stood and pulled out the syringe that would send him off to dreamland. Holding the needle in the air and letting the drug spurt out from the end would have more impact on him, but she had to draw the line on her theatrics somewhere.

Realization dawned on his face, and he shook his head violently. "No, Glen. Don't do this. You can't do this." He tried to back away from her, but the restraints held him in place. "Please don't kill me."

Glenda laughed. "I'm pretty sure you want to be dead when I skin you. I don't have those types of painkillers with me."

She stepped to the edge of the bed, and he squirmed around, howling like she was trying to skin him right here, but he couldn't move.

"Help me?" he screamed, voice growing louder, more desperate. "Please, someone help me?"

Glenda raised the syringe so he could see it. "This will go so much easier if you hold still."

She shouldn't be enjoying this, but she was. Just like when she's cut off Shannon's head, who'd been dead of course. All those years she had begged and pleaded with Gus to leave her friends alone, to not break their hearts and dump them. To not make them hate her. None of that had worked.

And his begging wouldn't work with her now.

She flipped off the blanket to uncover his bare leg, and he did a double-take. He probably hadn't realized that last night she'd put him in shorts.

Glenda and Gus

She would rather give him the shot in his fleshy butt, but with him twisting and trying to turn, the butt wouldn't work. So the leg it was.

He squealed and squirmed and cried. "Glen, no. Please don't."

She quickly administered the shot and stepped back.

"Fuck you, Glen. Fuck you, fuck you!" His bloodshot eyes shot fire at her along with his vulgar words. "You're gonna pay for this, you fucking bitch."

"Did you kiss your girlfriend with that nasty mouth?" Glenda laughed. But really, this noise was grating on her ears. And the smell. He'd pissed himself once again.

Glenda stood just out of reach as he writhed on the bed. "Here, maybe this will help," she said. "Glenda and Gus. Gus and Glenda. Built-in best friends to last for-ev-eh."

She kept singing until his voice turned from cursing to grunts and moans, until the movements slowed, until he collapsed on his pillows, his whole body red as if on fire. She wanted their last few hours together to be peaceful, so she could talk and share and remember the good times.

Suzi Wieland

Yes, she hated Gus, but she also loved him. He was her twin. They had a bond that could not be broken. Not even in death.

So she would talk to him about the good days, the good memories before he'd turned into a jerk and hurt her and so many other women. She'd tell the stories about the games they'd played as children, their bike-ride adventures, and the hours they spent at the playground.

She would tell him that she loved him.

And then she'd give him the shot to stop his heart.

Chapter Six

Glenda sighed at the mount sitting next to the stone fireplace. The pallid skin, the unsightly black seams. It didn't look any better now that she'd moved it inside the house. All the research she done online had been right: trying to taxidermy a human just didn't work.

Gus did not look like himself.

Yes, she'd known he wouldn't exactly, but he *really* didn't look like himself. She's tried so hard, but being this was her first taxidermy project, and well, since Gus didn't have any fur or feathers that covered up those ugly seams, it was the best she could do.

Her best wasn't good enough though. She couldn't live with this ugly thing in her peaceful home.

Suzi Wieland

Thanks, Gus. She rolled her eyes at him and lifted her feet to the small ottoman in front of her couch. He made life difficult, whether he was dead or alive.

She didn't really need him here in the living room anyway. She could still feel their bond if she buried him outside, and next spring he'd fertilize her garden. All she had to do was clear out a few more trees off to the side, and it'd be the perfect spot for a garden, catching most of the sun until later afternoon.

Glenda stared at his grotesque face, which matched the person he'd truly been, but despite all the bad choices and ugliness inside him, she still loved him.

Glenda and Gus. Gus and Glenda. Built-in best friends to last for-ev-eh.

Okay, maybe not forever, but maybe for a week or so. Then she'd bury that horrid thing in the ground.

Acknowledgments

Thank you to Theresa Paolo and Cassie Mae and all my writing friends for help with covers and blurbs and everything else. Thank you also to Kary Nelson for helping with my medical questions.

About the Author

Reading has always been a big part of Suzi's life. She even won the most-pages-read award a few times in her junior high English class, many years ago. She started several writing projects as a kid but never actually finished anything, and then she took a big break from writing that lasted well into adulthood.

She's written in a variety of genres, including horror, thriller, and women's fiction, and has even dipped into fantasy slightly with her fairy tale retellings. She has also published contemporary young adult stories under the name Suzi Drew.

Her non-writing life includes her family and friends, her sweet and fluffy dog, and an awesome job editing fiction with some of her writer friends. (Oh wait, that's still a part of writing. Seems she can't get away from the written word!)

To find out more about Suzi,
go to SuziWieland.com.

Also by Suzi Wieland

<u>Thriller Novels</u>
Black Diamond Dogs

<u>Horror Novels</u>
House of Desire

<u>Horror/Suspense Novellas and Shorts</u>
Shallow Depths
(Un)lucky Thirteen
Long-Term Effects
The Silent Treatment

Twisted Twins Series
Glenda and Gus
Two for the Price of One
A Hard Split

<u>Fairy Tale Novellas</u>
The Down the Twisted Path Series
In the Queen's Dark Light
When the Forest Cries
Killing Rosie
The Perfect Meal
An Unwanted Life
The Whole Story

Please visit SuziWieland.com
for more information.

www.ingramcontent.com/pod-product-compliance
Lightning Source LLC
LaVergne TN
LVHW041714060526
838201LV00043B/733